Six Chicks

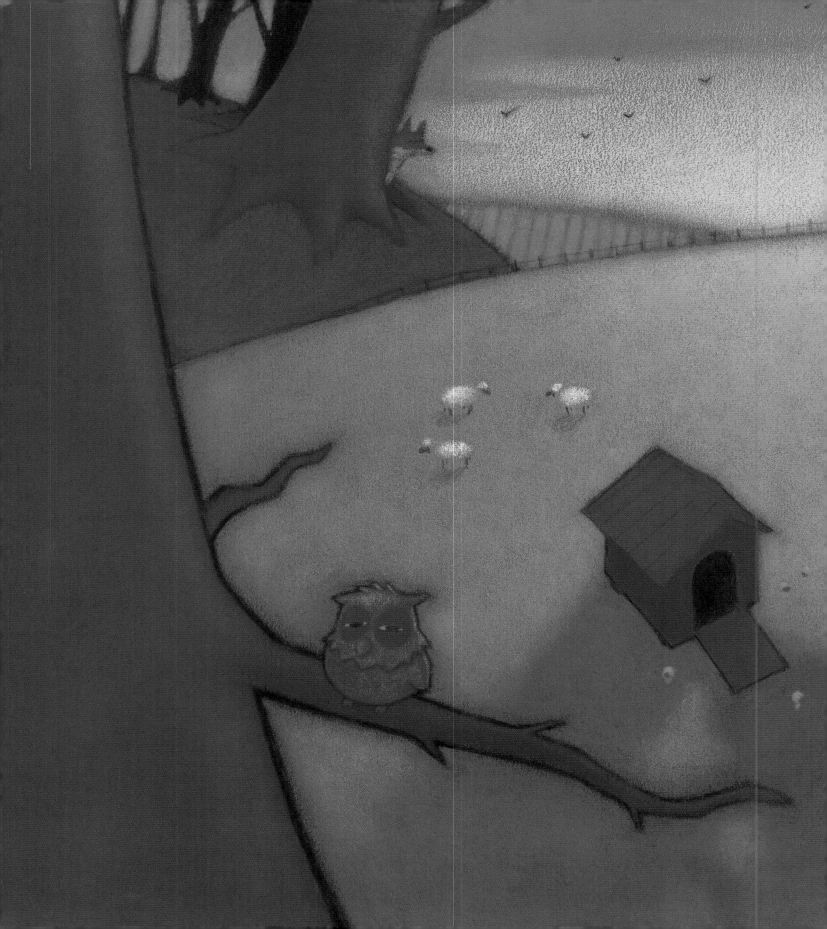

Six Chicks

Henrietta Branford

ILLUSTRATED BY
Thierry Elfezzani

Collins

An imprint of HarperCollinsPublishers

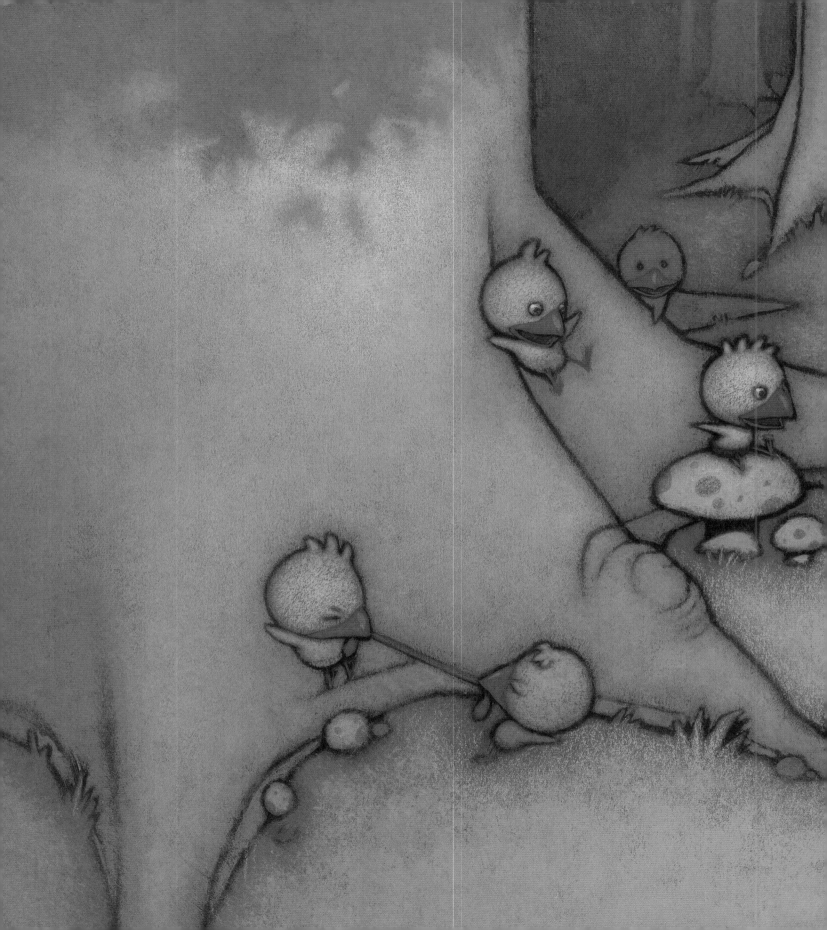

Red Hen is settling *six chicks* off to bed.

First she sings them six songs,
sweet and low.
Six chicks sing along softly.

But only one chick goes to sleep.

Red Hen chats cheerfully for a while.

Then she kisses *five chicks* on the cheek.

Five chicks snuggle down to snooze.

But only one more chick goes to sleep.

Red Hen tells four fine stories
about foolish fox and the clever chickens.
Four chicks chuckle.

But only one more chick goes to sleep.

Red Hen fetches three soft shawls and
tucks **three chicks** up cosy and warm.
Three chicks snore softly.

But only one more chick goes to sleep.

Red Hen wraps two chicks
in a rug and rocks them.
Two chicks rock along with Red Hen.

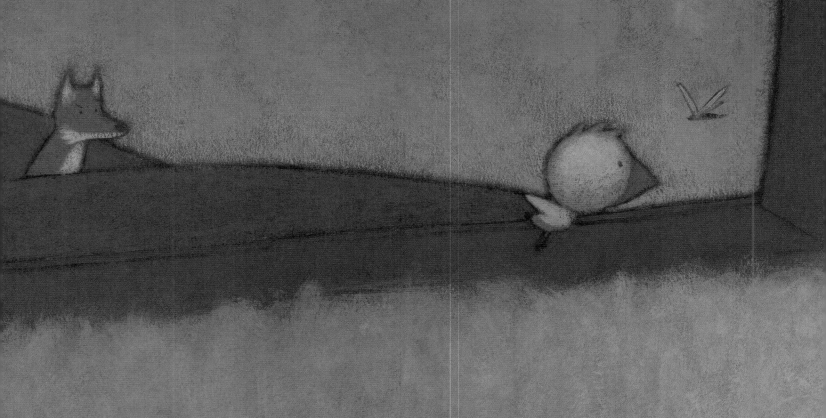

But only one more chick goes to sleep.

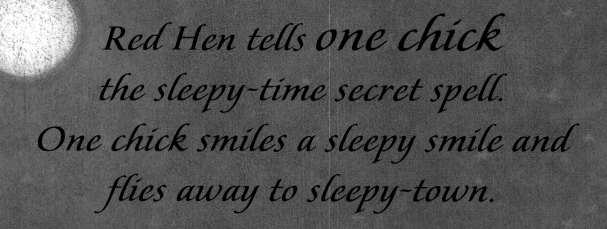

Red Hen tells one chick
the sleepy-time secret spell.
One chick smiles a sleepy smile and
flies away to sleepy-town.

At last. Six chicks, all asleep.

And one Red Hen.

First published in Great Britain by HarperCollins Publishers Ltd in 2004

1 3 5 7 9 10 8 6 4 2

ISBN: 978-0-00-783801-1

The HarperCollins website address is: www.harpercollins.co.uk

Printed and bound in Malaysia